In
1935 if you wanted to
read a good book, you needed
either a lot of money or a library card.
Cheap paperbacks were available, but their
poor production generally mirrored the quality
between the covers. One weekend that year,
Allen Lane, Managing Director of The Bodley Head,
having spent the weekend visiting Agatha Christie,
found himself on a platform at Exeter station trying to
find something to read for his journey back to London.
He was appalled by the quality of the material he had to
choose from. Everything that Allen Lane achieved from that
day until his death in 1970 was based on a passionate belief
in the existence of 'a vast reading public for *intelligent*
books at a low price'. The result of his momentous vision
was the birth not only of Penguin, but of the 'paperback
revolution'. Quality writing became available for the price of
a packet of cigarettes, literature became a mass medium
for the first time, a nation of book-borrowers became a
nation of book-buyers – and the very concept of book
publishing was changed for ever. Those founding
principles – of quality and value, with an overarching
belief in the fundamental importance of reading –
have guided everything the company has
done since 1935. Sir Allen Lane's
pioneering spirit is still very much alive
at Penguin in 2005. Here's to
the next 70 years!

MORE THAN A BUSINESS

'We decided it was time to end the almost customary half-hearted manner in which cheap editions were produced – as though the only people who could possibly want cheap editions must belong to a lower order of intelligence. We, however, believed in the existence in this country of a vast reading public for intelligent books at a low price, and staked everything on it'
Sir Allen Lane, 1902–1970

'The Penguin Books are splendid value for sixpence, so splendid that if other publishers had any sense they would combine against them and suppress them'
George Orwell

'More than a business … a national cultural asset'
Guardian

'When you look at the whole Penguin achievement you know that it constitutes, in action, one of the more democratic successes of our recent social history'
Richard Hoggart

Iron Potassium Nickel

PRIMO LEVI

PENGUIN BOOKS

PENGUIN BOOKS

Published by the Penguin Group
Penguin Books Ltd, 80 Strand, London WC2R ORL, England
Penguin Group (USA) Inc., 375 Hudson Street, New York, New York 10014, USA
Penguin Group (Canada), 10 Alcorn Avenue, Toronto, Ontario, Canada M4V 3B2
(a division of Pearson Penguin Canada Inc.)
Penguin Ireland, 25 St Stephen's Green, Dublin 2, Ireland
(a division of Penguin Books Ltd)
Penguin Group (Australia), 250 Camberwell Road, Camberwell, Victoria 3124,
Australia (a division of Pearson Australia Group Pty Ltd)
Penguin Books India Pvt Ltd, 11 Community Centre,
Panchsheel Park, New Delhi – 110 017, India
Penguin Group (NZ), cnr Airborne and Rosedale Roads, Albany,
Auckland 1310, New Zealand (a division of Pearson New Zealand Ltd)
Penguin Books (South Africa) (Pty) Ltd, 24 Sturdee Avenue,
Rosebank 2196, South Africa

Penguin Books Ltd, Registered Offices: 80 Strand, London WC2R ORL, England

www.penguin.com

The Periodic Table first published 1975
This translation first published in the USA by Shocken Books Inc. 1984
First published in Penguin Books 1985
This extract published as a Pocket Penguin 2005

1

Copyright © Giulio Einaudi Editore, s.p.a., Torino, 1975
Translation copyright © Shocken Books Inc., 1984
All rights reserved

Set in 11/13pt Monotype Dante
Typeset by Palimpsest Book Production Limited
Polmont, Stirlingshire
Printed in England by Clays Ltd, St Ives plc

Contents

Iron

Night lay beyond the walls of the Chemical Institute, the night of Europe: Chamberlain had returned from Munich duped, Hitler had marched into Prague without firing a shot, Franco had subdued Barcelona and was ensconced in Madrid. Fascist Italy, the small-time pirate, had occupied Albania, and the premonition of imminent catastrophe condensed like grumous dew in the houses and streets, in wary conversations and dozing consciences.

But the night did not penetrate those thick walls; Fascist censorship itself, the regime's masterwork, kept us shut off from the world, in a white, anesthetized limbo. About thirty of us had managed to surmount the harsh barrier of the first exams and had been admitted to the second year's Qualitative Analysis laboratory. We had entered that enormous, dark, smoky hall like someone who, coming into the House of the Lord, reflects on each of his steps. The previous lab, where I had tackled zinc, seemed an infantile exercise to us now, similar to when as children we had played at cooking: something, by hook or crook, in one way or another, always came of it, perhaps too little, perhaps not very pure, but you really had to be a hopeless case or pigheaded not to get magnesium sulfate from magnesite, or potassium bromide from bromine.

Not here: here the affair had turned serious, the confrontation with Mother-Matter, our hostile mother, was tougher and closer. At two in the afternoon, Professor D., with his ascetic and distracted air, handed each of us precisely one gram of a certain powder: by the next day we had to complete the qualitative analysis, that is, report what metals and nonmetals it contained. Report in writing, like a police report, only yes and no, because doubts and hesitations were not admissible: it was each time a choice, a deliberation, a mature and responsible undertaking, for which Fascism had not prepared us, and from which emanated a good smell, dry and clean.

Some elements, such as iron and copper, were easy and direct, incapable of concealment; others, such as bismuth and cadmium, were deceptive and elusive. There was a method, a toilsome, age-old plan for systematic research, a kind of combined steamroller and fine-toothed comb which nothing (in theory) could escape, but I preferred to invent each time a new road, with swift, extemporaneous forays, as in a war of movement, instead of the deadly grind of a war of position. Sublimate mercury into droplets, transform sodium into chloride, and identify it as trough-shaped chips under my microscope. One way or another, here the relationship with Matter changed, became dialectical: it was fencing, a face-to-face match. Two unequal opponents: on one side, putting the questions, the unfledged, unarmed chemist, at his elbow the textbook by Autenrieth as his sole ally (because D., often called to help out in difficult cases, maintained a scrupulous neutrality, refused to give an opinion: a wise attitude, since whoever opens his mouth can put his foot in it, and professors are not supposed to do that); on the other side, responding with enigmas, stood Matter, with her sly passivity, ancient as the All and portentously rich in deceptions, as solemn and subtle as the Sphinx. I was just beginning to read German words and was enchanted by the word *Urstoff* (which means 'element': literally, 'primal substance') and by the prefix *Ur* which appeared in it and which in fact expresses ancient origin, remote distance in space and time.

In this place, too, nobody wasted many words teaching us how to protect ourselves from acids, caustics, fires, and explosions; it appeared that the Institute's rough and ready morality counted on the process of natural selection to pick out those among us most qualified for physical and professional survival. There were few ventilation hoods; each student, following his text's prescriptions, in the course of systematic analysis, conscientiously let loose into the air a good dose of hydrochloric acid and ammonia, so that a dense, hoary mist of ammonium chloride stagnated permanently in the lab, depositing minute scintillating crystals on the windowpanes. Into the hydrogen sulfide room with its murderous atmosphere withdrew couples seeking privacy and a few lone wolves to eat their snacks.

Through the murk and in the busy silence, we heard a Piedmontese voice say: '*Nuntio vobis gaudium magnum. Habemus ferrum.'* 'I announce to you a great joy. We have iron.' It was March 1939, and a few days earlier an almost identical solemn announcement (*'Habemus Papam'*) had closed the conclave that had raised to Peter's Throne Cardinal Eugenio Pacelli, in whom many put their hopes, since one must after all put one's hope in someone or something. The blasphemous announcement came from Sandro, the quiet one.

In our midst, Sandro was a loner. He was a boy of medium height, thin but muscular, who never wore an overcoat, even on the coldest days. He came to class in worn corduroy knickers, knee socks made of homespun wool and sometimes a short black cape which made me think of the Tuscan poet Renato Fucini. He had large, calloused hands, a bony, rugged profile, a face baked by the sun, a low forehead beneath the line of his hair, which he wore very short and cut in a brush. He walked with the peasant's long, slow stride.

A few months before, the racial laws against the Jews had been proclaimed, and I too was becoming a loner. My Christian classmates were civil people; none of them, nor any of the teachers, had directed at me a hostile word or gesture, but I could feel them withdraw and, following an ancient pattern, I withdrew as well: every look exchanged between me and them was accompanied by a minuscule but perceptible flash of mistrust and suspicion. What do you think of me? What am I for you? The same as six months ago, your equal who does not go to Mass,

4

or the Jew who, as Dante put it, 'in your midst laughs at you'?

I had noticed with amazement and delight that something was happening between Sandro and me. It was not at all a friendship born from affinity; on the contrary, the difference in our origins made us rich in 'exchangeable goods,' like two merchants who meet after coming from remote and mutually unknown regions. Nor was it the normal, portentous intimacy of twenty-year-olds: with Sandro I never reached this point. I soon realized that he was generous, subtle, tenacious, and brave, even with a touch of insolence, but he had an elusive, untamed quality; so that, although we were at the age when one always has the need, instinct, and immodesty of inflicting on one another everything that swarms in one's head and elsewhere (and this is an age that can last long, but ends with the first compromise), nothing had gotten through his carapace of reserve, nothing of his inner world, which nevertheless one felt was dense and fertile – nothing save a few occasional, dramatically truncated hints. He had the nature of a cat with whom one can live for decades without ever being permitted to penetrate its sacred pelt.

We had many concessions to make to each other. I told him we were like cation and anion, but Sandro did not seem to acknowledge the comparison. He was born in Serra d'Ivrea, a beautiful but niggardly region. He was the son of a mason and spent his summers working as a shepherd. Not a shepherd of souls: a shepherd of sheep, and not because of Arcadian rhetoric or eccentricity, but happily, out of love for the earth and grass and an abundance of heart. He had a curious mimetic talent, and when he talked about cows, chickens, sheep, and dogs he was transformed, imitating their way of looking, their movements and voices, becoming very gay and seeming to turn into an animal himself, like a shaman. He taught me about plants and animals, but said very little about his family. His father had died when he was a child; they were simple, poor people, and since the boy was bright, they had decided to make him study so that he would bring money home: he had accepted this with Piedmontese seriousness but without enthusiasm. He had traveled the long route of high school – *liceo* – aiming at the highest marks with the least effort. He was not interested in Catullus and Descartes, he was interested in being promoted, and spending Sunday on his skis and climbing the rocks. He had chosen chemistry because he had thought it better than other studies; it was a trade that dealt with things one can see and touch, a way to earn one's bread less tiring than working as a carpenter or a peasant.

We began studying physics together, and Sandro was surprised when I tried to explain to him some of the ideas that at the time I was confusedly cultivating. That the nobility of Man, acquired in a hundred centuries of trial and error, lay in making himself the conqueror of matter, and that I had enrolled in chemistry because I wanted to remain faithful to this nobility. That conquering matter is to understand it, and understanding matter is necessary to understanding the universe and ourselves: and that therefore Mendeleev's Periodic Table, which just during those weeks we were laboriously learning to unravel, was poetry, loftier and more solemn than all the poetry we had swallowed down in *liceo*; and come to think of it, it even rhymed! That if one looked for the bridge, the missing link, between the world of words and the world of things, one did not have to look far: it was there, in our Autenrieth, in our smoke-filled labs, and in our future trade.

And finally, and fundamentally, an honest and open boy, did he not smell the stench of Fascist truths which tainted the sky? Did he not perceive it as an ignominy that a thinking man should be asked to believe without thinking? Was he not filled with disgust at all the dogmas, all the unproved affirmations, all the imperatives? He did feel it; so then, how could he not feel a new dignity and majesty in our study, how could he ignore the fact that the chemistry and physics on which we fed, besides being in themselves nourishments vital in themselves, were the antidote to Fascism which he and I were seeking, because they were clear and distinct and verifiable at every step, and not a tissue of lies and emptiness, like the radio and newspapers?

Sandro listened to me with ironical attention, always ready to deflate me with a couple of civil and terse words when I trespassed into rhetoric. But something was ripening in him (certainly not all my doing; those were months heavy with fateful events), something that troubled him because it was at once new and ancient. He, who until then had read only Salgari, Jack London, and Kipling, overnight became a furious reader: he digested and remembered everything, and everything in him spontaneously fell into place as a way of life; together with this, he began to study, and his average shot up from C to A. At the same time, out of unconscious gratitude, and perhaps also out of a desire to get even, he in turn took an interest in my education and made it clear to me that it had gaps. I might even be right: it might be that Matter is our teacher and perhaps also, for lack of something better, our political school; but he had another form of matter to lead me to, another teacher: not the powders of the Analytical Lab but the true, authentic, timeless *Urstoff*, the rocks and ice of the nearby mountains. He proved to me without too much difficulty that I didn't have the proper credentials to talk about matter. What commerce, what intimacy had I had, until then, with Empedocles' four elements? Did I know how to light a stove? Wade across a torrent? Was I familiar with a storm high up in the mountains? The sprouting of seeds? No. So he too had something vital to teach me.

A comradeship was born, and there began for me a feverish season. Sandro seemed to be made of iron, and he was bound to iron by an ancient kinship: his father's fathers, he told me, had been tinkers (*magnín*) and blacksmiths in the Canavese valleys: they made nails on the charcoal forges, sheathed wagon wheels with red-hot hoops, pounded iron plates until deafened by the noise; and he himself when he saw the red vein of iron in the rock felt he was meeting a friend. In the winter when it suddenly hit him, he would tie his skis on his rusty bike, leaving early in the morning and pedaling away until he reached the snow, without a cent, an artichoke in one pocket and the other full of lettuce; then he came back in the evening or even the next day, sleeping in haylofts, and the more storms and hunger he suffered the happier and healthier he was.

In the summer, when he went off by himself, he often took along a dog to keep him company. This was a small yellow mongrel with a downcast expression; in fact, as Sandro had told me, acting out in his way the animal episode, as a puppy he had had a mishap with a cat. He had come too close to a litter of newborn kittens, the mother cat was miffed and became enraged, and had begun to hiss, getting all puffed up; but the puppy had not yet learned the meaning of those signals and remained there like a fool. The cat had attacked him, chased him, caught him, and scratched his nose; the dog had been permanently traumatized. He felt dishonored, and so Sandro had made him a cloth ball, explained to him that it was the cat, and every morning presented it to him so that he could take his revenge on it for the insult and regain his canine honor. For the same therapeutic motive, Sandro took him to the mountains, so he could have some fun: he tied him to one end of a rope, tied himself to the other, set the dog firmly on a rock ledge, and then climbed up; when the rope ended, he pulled it up slowly, and the dog had learned to walk up with his muzzle pointed skywards and his four paws against the nearly vertical wall of rock, moaning softly as though he were dreaming.

Sandro climbed the rocks more by instinct than technique, trusting to the strength of his hands and saluting ironically, in the projecting rock to which he clung, the silicon, calcium, and magnesium he had learned to recognize in the course on mineralogy. He seemed to feel that he had wasted a day if he had not in some way gotten to the bottom of his reserve of energy, and then even his eyes became brighter and he explained to me that, with a sedentary life, a deposit of fat forms behind the eyes, which is not healthy; by working hard the fat is consumed and the eyes sink back into their sockets and become keener.

He spoke grudgingly about his exploits. He did not belong to that species of persons who do things in order to talk about them (like me); he did not like high-sounding words, indeed words. It appeared that in speaking, as in mountain climbing, he had never received lessons; he spoke as no one speaks, saying only the core of things.

If necessary he carried a thirty-kilo pack, but usually he traveled without it; his pockets were sufficient, and in them he put some vegetables, as I have said, a chunk of bread, a pocketknife, sometimes the dog-eared Alpine Club guide, and a skein of wire for emergency repairs. In fact he did not carry the guide because he believed in it, but for the opposite reason. He rejected it because he felt that it shackled him; not only that, he also saw it as a bastard creature, a detestable hybrid of snow and rock mixed up with paper. He took it into the mountains to vilify. Happy if he could catch it in an error, even if it was at his and his climbing companion's expense. He could walk for two days without eating, or eat three meals all together and then leave. For him, all seasons were good. In the winter he skied, but not at the well-equipped, fashionable slopes, which he shunned with laconic scorn: too poor to buy ourselves the sealskin strips for the ascents, he showed me how you sew on rough hemp cloths, Spartan devices which absorb the water and then freeze like codfish, and must be tied around your waist when you ski downhill. He dragged me along on exhausting treks through the fresh snow, far from any sign of human life, following routes that he seemed to intuit like a savage. In the summer, from shelter to shelter, inebriating ourselves with the sun, the effort, and the wind, and scraping the skin of our fingertips on rocks never before touched by human hands: but not on the famous peaks, nor in quest of memorable feats; such things did not matter to him at all. What mattered was to know his limitations, to test and improve himself; more obscurely, he felt the need to prepare himself (and to prepare me) for an iron future, drawing closer month by month.

To see Sandro in the mountains reconciled you to

the world and made you forget the nightmare weighing on Europe. This was his place, what he had been made for, like the marmots whose whistle and snout he imitated: in the mountains he became happy, with a silent, infectious happiness, like a light that is switched on. He aroused a new communion with the earth and sky, into which flowed my need for freedom, the plenitude of my strength, and a hunger to understand the things he had pushed me toward. We would come out at dawn, rubbing our eyes, through the small door of the Martinotti bivouac, and there, all around us, barely touched by the sun, stood the white and brown mountains, new as if created during the night that had just ended and at the same time innumerably ancient. They were an island, an elsewhere.

In any event, it was not always necessary to go high and far. In the in-between seasons Sandro's kingdom was the rock gymnasiums. There are several, two or three hours by bike from Turin, and I would be curious to know whether they are still frequented: the Straw Stack Pinnacles with the Wolkmann Tower, the Teeth of Cumiana, Patanüa Rock (which means Bare Rock), the Plô, the Sbarüa, and others, with their homely, modest names. The last, the Sbarüa, I think was discovered by Sandro himself and a mythical brother of his whom Sandro never let me see but who, from his few scanty hints, must have stood in the same relationship to him as he stood to the run of humanity. Sbarüa is a noun from the verb 'sbarüé', which means 'to terrify'; the

Sbarüa is a prism of granite that towers about a hundred meters above a modest hill bristling with brambles and a brushwood coppice; like Dante's Veglio di Creta – the Old Man of Crete – it is split from base to summit by a fissure that gets narrower as it rises, finally forcing the climber to come out on the rock face itself, where, precisely, he is terrified, and where at that time there was just a single piton, charitably left behind by Sandro's brother.

Those were curious places, frequented by a few dozen amateurs of our stamp, all of whom Sandro knew either by name or sight: we climbed up, not without technical problems, and surrounded by the irritating buzz of enormous bluebottle flies attracted by our sweat, crawling up good solid rock walls interrupted by grassy ledges where ferns and strawberries grew or, in the fall, blackberries: often enough we used as holds the trunks of puny little trees, rooted in the cracks, and after a few hours we reached the peak, which was not a peak at all but mostly placid pastureland where cows stared at us with indifferent eyes. Then we descended at breakneck speed, in a few minutes, along paths strewn with old and recent cow dung, to recover our bikes.

At other times our exploits were more demanding; never any quiet jaunts, since Sandro said that we would have plenty of time when we were forty to look at the scenery. 'Let's go, shall we?' he said to me one day in February – which in his language meant that, since the weather was good, we should leave in the afternoon for the winter climb of the

Tooth of M., which for some weeks had been one of our projects. We slept in an inn and left the next day, not too early, at some undetermined hour (Sandro did not like watches: he felt their quiet continuous admonishment to be an arbitrary intrusion). We plunged boldly into the fog and came out of it about one o'clock, in gleaming sunlight and on the big crest of a peak which was not the right one.

I then said that we should be able to go down about a hundred meters, cross over halfway up the mountain, and go up along the next ridge; or, better yet, since we were already there, continue climbing and be satisfied with the wrong peak, which in any case was only forty meters lower than the right one. But Sandro, with splendid bad faith, said in a few dense syllables that my last proposal was fine, but from there 'by way of the easy northwest ridge' (this was a sarcastic quotation from the abovementioned Alpine Club guide) we could also reach the Tooth of M. in half an hour; and what was the point of being twenty if you couldn't permit yourself the luxury of taking the wrong route.

The easy ridge must really have been easy, indeed elementary in the summer; but we found it in a very discomforting state. The rock was wet on the side facing the sun and covered with a black layer of ice in the shade; between one large outcrop of rock and another lay pockets of melting snow into which we sank to our waists. We reached the top at five; I dragged myself along so pitifully that it was painful, while Sandro was seized by a sinister hilarity that I found very annoying.

'And how do we get down?'

'As for getting down, we shall see,' he replied, and added mysteriously: 'The worst that can happen is to have to taste bear meat.' Well, we tasted bear meat in the course of that night, which seemed very, very long. We got down in two hours, helped badly by the rope, which was frozen; it had become a malignant, rigid tangle that snagged on each projection and rang against the rock face like the cable of a funicular. At seven we were on the bank of a frozen pond and it was dark. We ate the little that was left, built a useless dry stone wall facing the wind, and lay down on the ground to sleep, pressed to each other. It was as though time itself had frozen; every so often we got to our feet to reactivate our circulation, and it was always the same time: the wind never stopped blowing, there was always the same ghost of a moon, always at the same point in the sky, and in front of the moon passed a fantastic cavalcade of tattered clouds, always the same. We had taken off our shoes, as described in Lammer's books, so dear to Sandro, and we kept our feet in our packs; at the first funereal light, which seemed to seep from the snow and not the sky, we rose with our limbs benumbed and our eyes glittering from lack of sleep, hunger, and the hardness of our bed. And we found our shoes so frozen that they rang like bells, and to get them on we had to hatch them out like brood hens.

But we went back down to the valley under our

own steam; and to the innkeeper who asked us, with a snicker, how things had gone, and meanwhile was staring at our wild, exalted faces, we answered flippantly that we had had an excellent outing, then paid the bill and departed with dignity. This was it – the bear meat; and now that many years have passed, I regret that I ate so little of it, for nothing has had, even distantly, the taste of that meat, which is the taste of being strong and free, free also to make mistakes and be the master of one's destiny. That is why I am grateful to Sandro for having led me consciously into trouble, on that trip and other undertakings which were only apparently foolish, and I am certain that they helped me later on.

They didn't help Sandro, or not for long. Sandro was Sandro Delmastro, the first man to be killed fighting in the Resistance with the Action Party's Piedmontese Military Command. After a few months of extreme tension, in April of 1944 he was captured by the Fascists, did not surrender, and tried to escape from the Fascist Party house in Cuneo. He was killed with a tommygun burst in the back of the neck by a monstrous child-executioner, one of those wretched murderers of fifteen whom Mussolini's Republic of Salò recruited in the reformatories. His body was abandoned in the road for a long time, because the Fascists had forbidden the population to bury him.

Today I know that it is a hopeless task to try to dress a man in words, make him live again on the printed page, especially a man like Sandro. He was not the sort of person you can tell stories about, nor to whom one erects monuments – he who laughed at all monuments: he lived completely in his deeds, and when they were over nothing of him remains – nothing but words, precisely.

Potassium

In January 1941 the fate of Europe and the world seemed to be sealed. Only the deluded could still think that Germany would not win; the stolid English 'had not noticed that they had lost the game,' and obstinately resisted under the bombings; but they were alone and suffered bloody losses on all fronts. Only a voluntarily deaf and blind man could have any doubts about the fate reserved for the Jews in a German Europe: we had read Feuchtwanger's *Oppermanns*, smuggled secretly in from France, and a British White Book, which arrived from Palestine and described the 'Nazi atrocities'; we had only believed half of it, but that was enough. Many refugees from Poland and France had reached Italy, and we had talked with them: they did not know the details of the slaughters that were taking place behind a monstrous curtain of silence, but each of them was a messenger, like those who run to Job to tell him, 'I alone have escaped to tell you the story.'

And yet, if we wanted to live, if we wished in some way to take advantage of the youth coursing through our veins, there was indeed no other resource than self-imposed blindness; like the English, 'we did not notice,' we pushed all dangers into the limbo of things not perceived or immediately forgotten. We could also, in the abstract, throw everything away and escape and be transplanted to some remote, mythical country, chosen from among the few that kept their frontiers open: Madagascar, British Honduras. But to do this one needed a lot of money and a fabulous capacity for initiative – and I, my family, and our friends had neither one nor the other. Besides, if looked at from close by and in detail, things did not after all seem so disastrous: the Italy around us, or, to put it more accurately (at a time when one traveled little), Piedmont and Turin were not hostile. Piedmont was our true country, the one in which we recognized ourselves; the mountains around Turin, visible on clear days, and within reach of a bicycle, were ours, irreplaceable, and had taught us fatigue, endurance, and a certain wisdom. In short, our roots were in Piedmont and Turin, not enormous but deep, extensive, and fantastically intertwined.

Neither in us nor, more generally, in our generation, whether 'Aryan' or Jew, had the idea yet gained ground that one must and could resist Fascism. Our resistance at the time was passive and was limited to rejection, isolation, and avoiding contamination. The seed of active struggle had not survived down to us, it had been stifled a few years before with the final sweep of the scythe, which had relegated to prison, house arrest, exile, or silence the last Turinese protagonists and witnesses – Einaudi, Ginzburg, Monti, Vittorio Foa, Zini, Carlo Levi. These names said nothing to us, we knew hardly anything about them – the Fascism around us did not have opponents. We had to begin from scratch, 'invent' our anti-Fascism, create it from the germ, from the roots, from our roots. We looked around us and traveled up roads that led not very far away. The Bible, Croce, geometry, and physics seemed to us sources of certainty.

We gathered in the gym of the Talmud Torah – in the School of the Law, as the very old Hebrew elementary school was proudly called – and taught each other to find again in the Bible justice and injustice and the strength that overcomes injustice; to recognize the new oppressors in Ahasuerus and Nebuchadnezzar. But where was Kadosh Barukhú, 'the Saint, Blessed be He': he who breaks the slaves' chains and submerges the Egyptians' chariots? He who dictated the Law to Moses, and inspired the liberators Ezra and Nehemiah, no longer inspired anyone; the sky above us was silent and empty: he allowed the Polish ghettos to be exterminated, and slowly, confusedly, the idea was making headway in us that we were alone, that we had no allies we could count on, neither on earth nor in heaven, that we would have to find in ourselves the strength to resist. Therefore the impulse that drove us to explore our limits was not completely absurd: to travel hundreds of kilometers on our bikes, to climb with fury and patience up rock walls that we did not know very well, to subject ourselves voluntarily to hunger, cold, and fatigue, to train ourselves to endure and to make decisions. A piton goes in or it doesn't; the rope holds or it doesn't: these too were sources of certainty.

Chemistry, for me, had stopped being such a source. It led to the heart of Matter, and Matter was our ally precisely because the Spirit, dear to Fascism, was our enemy; but, having reached the fourth year of Pure Chemistry, I could no longer ignore the fact that chemistry itself, or at least that which we were being administered, did not answer my questions. To prepare phenyl bromide or methyl violet according to Gattermann was amusing, even exhilarating, but not very much different from following Artusi's recipes. Why in that particular way and not in another? After having been force fed in *liceo* the truths revealed by Fascist Doctrine, all revealed, unproven truths either bored me stiff or aroused my suspicion. Did chemistry theorems exist? No: therefore you had to go further, not be satisfied with the *quia*, go back to the origins, to mathematics and physics. The origins of chemistry were ignoble, or at least equivocal: the dens of the alchemists, their abominable hodgepodge of ideas and language, their confessed interest in gold, their Levantine swindles typical of charlatans or magicians; instead, at the origin of physics lay the strenuous clarity of the West – Archimedes and Euclid. I would become a physicist, *ruat coelum*: perhaps without a degree, since Hitler and Mussolini forbade it.

A brief course of exercises in physics formed part of the fourth-year chemistry program: simple measurements of viscosity, surface tension, rotatory power, and suchlike exercises. The course was conducted by a young assistant, thin, tall, a bit hunched over, polite, and extraordinarily shy, who behaved in a way that we were not used to. Our other teachers, almost without exception, showed themselves convinced of the importance and excellence of the subject they taught; some of them were in good faith, for others it was evidently a matter of personal supremacy, of their private hunting grounds. That assistant, however, almost had the air of apologizing to us, of ranging himself on our side: in his somewhat embarrassed and well-bred ironic smile, one seemed to read: 'I too know that with this antiquated and worn-out equipment you'll not be able to put together anything useful, and that furthermore these are all marginal futilities, and knowledge lives elsewhere; but this is a trade that you and I too must work at – so please try not to do much damage and to learn as much as you can.' In short, all the girls in the course fell in love with him.

During the span of those months I made desperate attempts to be taken on as a student assistant by this or that professor. Some of them snidely or even arrogantly told me that the racial laws prohibited it; others fell back on hazy or flimsy excuses. After having imperturbably collected the fourth or fifth rejection, I was going home one evening on my bike, with an almost palpable load of disheartenment and bitterness on my back. I was pedaling listlessly up Via Valperga Caluso, while from the Valentino Park gusts of freezing wind overtook and passed me; it was night by now, and the light of the street lamps, covered with purple for the blackout, did not prevail over the mist and darkness. The passersby were few and hurried; and then suddenly one among them caught my attention. He was going in my direction with a long, slow stride, he wore a long black over-coat, and his head was bare. He was walking a bit hunched over and looked like the assistant – it was the assistant. I passed him, uncertain as to what I should do; then I plucked up my courage, went back, and once again did not dare speak to him. What did I know about him? Nothing. He could be indifferent, a hypocrite, even an enemy. Then I thought that I risked nothing but another rejection, and without beating around the bush I asked him whether it would be possible to be accepted for experimental work in his school. The assistant looked at me with surprise; and instead of going into the long explana-tion I expected, he replied with two words from the Gospel: 'Follow me.'

The inside of the Institute of Experimental Physics was full of dust and century-old ghosts. There were rows of glass-doored cupboards packed with slips of paper, yellowed and gnawed by mice and paper moths: these were the observations of eclipses, regis-trations of earthquakes, meteorological bulletins from well into the last century. Along the walls of one corridor I found an extraordinary trumpet, more than thirty feet long, whose origin, purpose, and use no one any longer knew – perhaps it was to announce the Day of Judgment, when all that which is hidden will appear. There was an Aeolipyle in Secession style, a Hero's fountain, and a whole obsolete and prolix fauna of contraptions for generations destined for classroom demonstrations: a pathetic and ingenuous form of minor physics, in which stage setting counts for more than concept. It is neither illusionism nor conjuring trick but borders on them.

The assistant welcomed me in the tiny room on the ground floor where he himself lived, and which was bristling with a much different sort of equipment, unknown and exciting enthusiasm. Some molecules are carriers of an electrical dipole; they behave in short in an electrical field like minuscule compass needles: they orient themselves, some more sluggishly, others less so. Depending on conditions, they obey certain laws with greater or less respect. Well, now, these devices served to clarify those conditions and that inadequate respect. They were waiting for someone to put them to use; he was busy with other matters (astrophysics, he specified, and the information shook me to the marrow: so I had an astrophysicist right in front of me, in flesh and blood!) and besides he had no experience with certain manipulations which were considered necessary to purify the products that had to be measured; for this a chemist was necessary, and I was the welcomed chemist. He willingly handed over the field to me and the instruments. The field was two square meters of a table and desk; the instruments, a small family, but the most important were the Westphal balance and the heterodyne. The first I already knew; with the second I soon established a friendship. In substance it was a radio-receiving apparatus, built to reveal the slightest differences in frequency; and in fact, it went howlingly out of tune and barked like a watchdog simply if the operator shifted in his chair or moved a hand, or if someone just came into the room. Besides, at certain hours of the day, it revealed a whole intricate universe of mysterious messages, Morse tickings, modulated hisses, and deformed, mangled human voices, which pronounced sentences in incomprehensible languages, or others in Italian, but they were senseless sentences, in code. It was the radiophonic Babel of the war, messages of death transmitted by ships or planes from God knows who to God knows whom, beyond the mountains and the sea.

Beyond the mountains and the sea, the assistant explained to me, there was a scholar named Onsager, about whom he knew nothing except that he had worked out an equation that claimed to describe the behavior of polar molecules under all conditions, provided that they were in a liquid state. The equation functioned well for diluted solutions; it did not appear that anyone had bothered to verify it for concentrated solutions, pure polar liquids, and mixtures of the latter. This was the work that he proposed I do, to prepare a series of complex liquids and check if they obeyed Onsager's equation, which I accepted with indiscriminate enthusiasm. As a first step, I would have to do something he did not know how to do: at that time it was not easy to find pure products for analysis, and I was supposed to devote myself for a few weeks to purifying benzene, chlorobenzene, chlorophenols, aminophenols, toluidines, and more.

A few hours of contact were sufficient for the assistant's personality to become clearly defined. He was thirty, was recently married, came from Trieste but was of Greek origin, knew four languages, loved music, Huxley, Ibsen, Conrad, and Thomas Mann, the last so dear to me. He also loved physics, but he was suspicious of every activity that set itself a goal: therefore, he was nobly lazy and, naturally, detested Fascism.

His relationship to physics perplexed me. He did not hesitate to harpoon my last hippogriff, confirming quite explicitly that message about 'marginal futility' which we had read in his eyes in the lab. Not only those humble exercises of ours but physics as a whole was marginal, by its nature, by vocation, insofar as it set itself the task of regulating the universe of appearances, whereas the truth, the reality, the intimate essence of things and man exist elsewhere, hidden behind a veil, or seven veils (I don't remember exactly). He was a physicist, more precisely an astrophysicist, diligent and eager but without illusions: the Truth lay beyond, inaccessible to our telescopes, accessible to the initiates. This was a long road which he was traveling with effort, wonderment, and profound joy. Physics was prose: elegant gymnastics for the mind, mirror of Creation, the key to man's dominion over the planet; but what is the stature of Creation, of man and the planet? His road was long and he had barely started up it, but I was his disciple: Did I want to follow him?

It was a terrifying request. To be the assistant's disciple was for me an enjoyment of every minute, a never before experienced bond, without shadows, rendered more intense by the certainty that the relationship was mutual: I, a Jew, excluded and made skeptical by recent upheavals, the enemy of violence but not yet caught up in the necessity of an opposed violence, I should be for him the ideal interlocutor, a white sheet on which any message could be inscribed.

I did not mount the new gigantic hippogriff which the assistant offered me. During those months the Germans destroyed Belgrade, broke the Greek resistance, invaded Crete from the air: that was the Truth, that was the Reality. There were no escape routes, or not for me. Better to remain on the Earth, playing with the dipoles for lack of anything better, purify benzene and prepare for an unknown but imminent and certainly tragic future. To purify benzene, then, under the conditions to which the war and the bombings had reduced the Institute was not an insignificant undertaking: the assistant declared that I had carte blanche, I could rummage everywhere from basement to attic, appropriate any instrument or product, but I could not buy anything, even he couldn't, it was a regime of absolute autarky.

In the basement I found a huge demijohn of technical benzene, at 95 percent purity, better than nothing, but the manuals prescribed rectifying it and then putting it through a final distillation in the presence of sodium, to free it from the last traces of humidity. To rectify means to distill by fractions, discarding the fractions that boil lower or higher than prescribed, and garnering the 'heart,' which must boil at a constant temperature: I found in the inexhaustible basement the necessary glassware, including one of those Vigreux distillation columns, as pretty as a piece of lace, the product of superhuman patience and ability on the part of the glass blower, but (be it said between us) of debatable efficiency; I made the double boiler with a small aluminum pot.

Distilling is beautiful. First of all, because it is a slow, philosophic, and silent occupation, which keeps you busy but gives you time to think of other things, somewhat like riding a bike. Then, because it involves a metamorphosis from liquid to vapor (invisible), and from this once again to liquid; but in this double journey, up and down, purity is attained, an ambiguous and fascinating condition, which starts with chemistry and goes very far. And finally, when you set about distilling, you acquire the consciousness of repeating a ritual consecrated by the centuries, almost a religious act, in which from imperfect material you obtain the essence, the *usia*, the spirit, and in the first place alcohol, which gladdens the spirit and warms the heart. I took two good days to obtain a fraction of satisfying purity: for this operation, since I had to work with an open flame, I had voluntarily exiled myself to a small room on the second floor, deserted and empty and far from any human presence.

Now I had to distill a second time in the presence of sodium. Sodium is a degenerated metal: it is indeed a metal only in the chemical significance of the word, certainly not in that of everyday language. It is neither rigid nor elastic; rather it is soft like wax; it is not shiny or, better, it is shiny only if preserved with maniacal care, since otherwise it reacts in a few instants with air, covering itself with an ugly rough rind: with even greater rapidity it reacts with water, in which it floats (a metal that floats!), dancing frenetically and developing hydrogen. I ransacked the entrails of the Institute in vain: like Ariosto's Astolfo on the Moon I found dozens of labeled ampules, hundreds of abstruse compounds, other vague anonymous sediments apparently untouched for generations, but not a sign of sodium. Instead I found a small phial of potassium: potassium is sodium's twin, so I grabbed it and returned to my hermitage.

I put in the flask of benzene a lump of potassium, 'as large as half a pea' – so said the manual – and diligently distilled the contents: toward the end of the operation I dutifully doused the flame, took apart the apparatus, let the small amount of liquid in the flask cool off a bit, and then with a long pointed stick skewered the 'half pea' of potassium and lifted it out.

Potassium, as I said, is sodium's twin, but it reacts with air and water with even greater energy: it is known to everyone (and was known also to me) that in contact with water it not only develops hydrogen but also ignites. So I handled my 'half pea' like a holy relic: I placed it on a piece of dry filter paper, wrapped it up in it, went down into the Institute's courtyard, dug out a tiny grave, and buried the little bedeviled corpse. I carefully tamped down the earth above it and went back up to my work.

I took the now empty flask, put it under a faucet, and turned on the water. I heard a rapid thump and from the neck of the flask came a flash of flame directed at the window that was next to the wash-basin and the curtains around it caught fire. While I was stumbling around looking for some even primitive means to extinguish it, the panels of the shutter began to blister and the room was now full of smoke. I managed to push over a chair and tear down the curtains; I threw them on the floor and stomped furiously on them, while the smoke half blinded me and my blood was throbbing violently in my temples.

When it was all over, when the incandescent tatters were extinguished, I remained standing there for a few minutes, weak and stunned, my knees turned to water, contemplating the vestiges of the disaster without seeing them. As soon as I got my breath back, I went to the floor below and told the assistant what had happened. If it is true that there is no greater sorrow than to remember a happy time in a state of misery, it is just as true that calling up a moment of anguish in a tranquil mood, seated quietly at one's desk, is a source of profound satisfaction.

The assistant listened to my account with polite attention but with a questioning look: Who had compelled me to embark on that voyage, and to distill benzene by going to so much trouble? In a way, it served me right: these are the things that happen to the profane, to those who dawdle and play before the portals of the temple instead of going inside. But he didn't say a word; he resorted for the occasion (unwillingly, as always) to the hierarchical distance and pointed out to me that an empty flask does not catch fire: so it must not have been empty. It must have contained, if nothing else, the vapor of the benzene, besides of course the air that came in through its neck. But one has never seen the vapor of benzene, when cold, catch fire by itself: only the potassium could have set fire to the mixture, and I had taken out the potassium. All of it?

All, I answered; but then I was visited by a doubt, returned to the scene of the accident, and found fragments of the flask still on the floor: on one of them, by looking closely, one could see, barely visible, a tiny white fleck. I tested it with phenolphthalein: it was basic, it was potassium hydroxide. The guilty party had been found: adhering to the glass of the flask there must have remained a minuscule particle of potassium, all that was needed to react with the water I had poured in and set fire to the benzene vapors.

The assistant looked at me with an amused, vaguely ironic expression: better not to do than to do, better to meditate than to act, better his astrophysics, the threshold of the Unknowable, than my chemistry, a mess compounded of stenches, explosions, and small futile mysteries. I thought of another moral, more down to earth and concrete, and I believe that every militant chemist can confirm it: that one must distrust the almost-the-same (sodium is almost the same as potassium, but with sodium nothing would have happened), the practically identical, the approximate, the or-even, all surrogates, and all patchwork. The differences can be small, but they can lead to radically different consequences, like a railroad's switch points; the chemist's trade consists in good part in being aware of these differences, knowing them close up, and foreseeing their effects. And not only the chemist's trade.

Nickel

I had in a drawer an illuminated parchment on which was written in elegant characters that on Primo Levi, of the Jewish race, had been conferred a degree in Chemistry summa cum laude. It was therefore a dubious document, half glory and half derision, half absolution and half condemnation. It had remained in that drawer since July 1941, and now we were at the end of November. The world was racing to catastrophe, and around me nothing was happening. The Germans had spread like a flood in Poland, Norway, Holland, France, and Yugoslavia and had penetrated the Russian steppes like a knife cutting through butter. The United States did not move to help the English, who remained alone. I could not find work and was wearing myself out looking for any sort of paid occupation; in the next room my father, prostrated by a tumor, was living his last months.

The doorbell rang – it was a tall, thin young man wearing the uniform of the Italian army, and I immediately recognized in him the figure of the messenger, the Mercury who guides souls, or, if one wishes, the annunciatory angel. In short, the person for whom everyone waits, whether he knows it or not, and who brings the heavenly message that changes your life for good or ill, you don't know which until he opens his mouth.

He opened his mouth, and he had a strong Tuscan accent and asked for Dr. Levi, who incredibly was myself (I still wasn't accustomed to the title), introduced himself urbanely, and offered me a job. Who had sent him to me? Another Mercury, Caselli, the inflexible custodian of another man's fame: that 'laude' on my diploma had actually served for something.

That I was a Jew the lieutenant apparently knew (in any event, my last name left little room for doubt), but it didn't seem to matter to him. Moreover, it seemed that the business somehow suited him, that he took a bitter and subtle pleasure in breaking the laws of racial separation – in short, he was secretly an ally and sought an ally in me.

The work he offered me was mysterious and quite fascinating. 'In some place' there was a mine, from which was taken 2 percent of some useful material (he didn't tell me what) and 98 percent of sterile material, which was piled up in a nearby valley. In this sterile material there was nickel; very little, but its price was so high that its recovery should be given some thought. He had an idea, in fact a cluster of ideas, but he was in the military service and had little free time. I was supposed to replace him, test his ideas in the lab, and then, if possible, together with him, realize them industrially. It was clear that this required my transfer to that 'some place,' which was then sketchily described. The transfer would take place under a double seal of secrecy. In the first place, for my protection, nobody should know my name nor my abominable origin, because the 'some place' was under the control of the military authorities; and in the second place, to protect his idea, I would have to swear on my honor not to mention it to anyone. Besides, it was clear that one secret would reinforce the other and that therefore, to a certain degree, my condition as an outcast couldn't have been more opportune.

What was his idea, and where was this 'some place'? The lieutenant bowed out there; until my final acceptance he could not tell me much, that was obvious. In any case, the idea consisted in an attack on the sterile material in a gaseous phase, and the 'some place' was a few hours' journey from Turin. I quickly consulted with my parents. They agreed: with my father's illness the house had an urgent need of money. As for me, I had not the slightest doubt: I felt sapped by my inactivity, certain of my chemistry, and eager to put it to the test. Besides, the lieutenant had aroused my curiosity and I liked him.

One could see that he wore the uniform with revulsion; his choice of me must not have been dictated solely by practical considerations. He talked about Fascism and the war with reticence and a sinister gaiety that I had no trouble interpreting. It was the ironic gaiety of a whole generation of Italians, intelligent and honest enough to reject Fascism, too skeptical to oppose it actively, too young to passively accept the tragedy that was taking shape and to despair of the future; a generation to which I myself would have belonged if the providential racial laws had not intervened to bring me to a precocious maturity and guide me in my choice.

The lieutenant acknowledged my consent and without wasting time gave me an appointment at the railroad station for the next day. Preparations? I didn't need very much: certainly no documents (I would begin work incognito, without a name or with a false name – we'd see about that later on); a few heavy suits (my climbing outfits would go very well), a shirt, books if I wished. As for the rest, no problem: I would find a heated room, a lab, regular meals with a family of workers, and my colleagues were good people with whom, however, he advised me not to become too intimate for obvious reasons.

We left, got off the train, and reached the mine after a climb of five kilometers surrounded by a forest sparkling with hoarfrost. The lieutenant, who was briskly businesslike, introduced me summarily to the director, a young, tall, vigorous engineer who was even more businesslike and who evidently had already been told about me. I was taken into the lab, where a singular creature awaited me: a rather rawboned girl of eighteen, with fiery red hair and green, slanting, mischievous, alert eyes. I learned that she would be my assistant.

During the meal which, exceptionally, was offered to me on the office's premises, the radio broadcast the news of the Japanese attack on Pearl Harbor and Japan's declaration of war on the United States. My

fellow diners (a number of clerks, besides the lieutenant) greeted the announcement in various ways:
some, and among these the lieutenant himself, with
reserve and cautious glances at me; others, with
worried comments; still others, belligerently insisting
on the by now proven invincibility of the Japanese
and German armies.

So the 'some place' had become localized in space,
without, however, losing any of its magic. Yes, all
mines are magical per se, and always have been. The
entrails of the earth swarm with gnomes, kobolds
(cobalt!), *nickel*, German 'little demon' or 'sprite,' and
from which we derive the word nickel, creatures who
can be generous and let you find a treasure beneath
the tip of your pickax, or deceive and bedazzle you,
making modest pyrites glitter like gold, or disguising
zinc in the garb of tin: and in fact, many are the
minerals whose names have roots that signify 'decep-
tion, fraud, bedazzlement.'

This mine too had its magic, its wild enchantment.
On a squat, bleak hill, all jagged rocks and stumps,
was sunk a cyclopean, cone-shaped gorge, an artificial
crater, four hundred meters in diameter: it was in every
way similar to the schematic representations of Hell
in the synoptic tables of Dante's *Divine Comedy*. Along
the encircling tiers, day by day, were exploded dynamite charges: the slope of the cone's walls was graded
at the indispensable minimum so that the material
shaken loose would roll down to the bottom but
without gaining too much speed. At the bottom, in
Lucifer's place, stood a ponderous rolling shutter;

beneath this was a shallow vertical pit which led into a long horizontal tunnel; this in turn debouched in the open air on the side of the hill, just above the mine's main building. In the tunnel an armored train shuttled back and forth: a small but powerful locomotive positioned the cars one by one under the shutter so that they could be filled, then dragged them out to look again at the stars.

The plant was built in a tier along the slope of the hill and beneath the tunnel's opening; in it the mineral was shattered in a huge crusher that the director described to me and demonstrated with almost childlike enthusiasm. It was a bell turned upside down, or, if one wished, the corolla of a bindweed, four meters in diameter and constructed of massive steel: at its center, suspended from above and guided from below, swung a gigantic clapper. The oscillation was slight, barely visible, but was enough to split in the blink of an eye the mass of rock which poured down from the train: the rocks were split, pressed together lower down, split again, and came out below in fragments as large as a man's head. The operation proceeded in the midst of an apocalyptic uproar, a cloud of dust which could be seen down on the plain. The material was crushed again until it became gravel, then dried out and sifted; and it wasn't difficult to figure out that the final purpose of that gigantic labor was to extract a miserable 2 percent of asbestos which was trapped in those rocks. All the rest, thousands of tons a day, was dumped at random into the valley.

Year after year, the valley was being filled by a slow avalanche of dust and gravel. The asbestos that still was in it made the mass of material slightly slippery, sluggishly sticky, like a glacier: the enormous gray tongue, dotted with blackish rocks, crept laboriously, ponderously downhill, about ten meters a year; it exerted so much pressure on the walls of the valley as to produce deep transverse fissures in the rock; yearly it moved a few inches several of the buildings erected too far down. I lived in one of them, called the 'submarine' precisely because of its quiet downward drift.

There was asbestos everywhere, like ashy snow. If you left a book for a few hours on the table and then picked it up, you found its profile in negative; the roofs were covered by a thick layer of dust, which on rainy days soaked through like a sponge, and then suddenly would slide and crash violently to the ground. The head foreman in the mine, called Antaeus, was an obese giant with a thick black beard who actually seemed to draw his strength from Mother Earth. He told me that, years before, a persistent rain had washed many tons of asbestos from the walls of the mine; the asbestos had accumulated at the bottom of the cone over the open valve, secretly setting like a plug. Nobody had attached much importance to the matter, but it had continued to rain, the cone acted as a funnel, a lake of twenty thousand cubic meters of water had formed over the plug, and still nobody had given the matter any thought. He, Antaeus, saw trouble coming and had insisted that the then director do something about it: being the good mine foreman that he was he favored a nice big dynamite charge exploded without ado on the bottom of the lake; but what with this and that, it might be dangerous, you could damage the valve, best to get the advice of the administrative council, nobody wanted to decide, and meanwhile the mine, with its malign genius, decided by itself.

While the wise men were deliberating, a dull roar was heard, the plug had given way, the water sank in the pit and tunnel, swept away the train with all its cars, and laid waste the plant. Antaeus showed me the marks left by the flood, a good two meters above the inclined plane.

The workers and miners (who in the local jargon were called 'minors') came from the neighboring villages, walking perhaps two hours over the mountain paths. The clerks lived on the spot. The plain was only five kilometers away, but for all purposes the mine was a small autonomous republic. At that time of rationing and black market there were no supply problems up there; nobody knew how this was, but everyone had everything. Many clerks had their own truck gardens, around the square villa that housed the offices; some of them even had chicken coops. Several times one clerk's chickens would invade the truck garden of another, damaging it, and this produced tiresome disputes and feuds, which were ill-suited to the serenity of the place and the director's curt, no-nonsense nature. He had cut through the tangle in a manner worthy of him: he had ordered a Flobert shotgun and hung it on a nail in his office. Anyone who from the window saw a foreign chicken scratching around in his truck garden had the right to take the shotgun and shoot it twice: but the chicken had to be caught in the act. If the chicken died on the field, the corpse belonged to the shooter; this was the law. During the first days after the ruling, there had been many dashes for the gun and shootings, while all those not involved bet on the outcome, but then the trespassing stopped.

Other marvelous stories were told to me, like the story about Signor Pistamiglio's dog. This Signor Pistamiglio, when I got there, had been gone for years, but his memory was still alive and, as often happens, had acquired a gilded patina of legend. So then this Signor Pistamiglio was an excellent section chief, no longer young, a bachelor, full of common sense, esteemed by all, and his dog was a very beautiful German shepherd, equally upright and esteemed.

There came a certain Christmas and four of the fattest turkeys in the town down in the valley disappeared. Too bad: thieves had been suspected, a fox, and that was the end of it. But another winter came and this time seven turkeys disappeared between November and December. The thefts were reported to the local carabinieri, but nobody would have ever solved the mystery if Signor Pistamiglio himself had not let slip one word too many one evening when he'd drunk a bit. The turkey thieves were the two of them, he and his dog. On Sunday he took his dog to the town, roamed about among the farms, and showed him which were the most beautiful and least guarded turkeys; case by case he explained to him the best strategy; then they came back to the mine and at night he would set him free, and the dog arrived invisibly, slithering along the walls like a real wolf, jumped over the fence around the chicken coop or dug a passage under it, killed the turkey silently, and brought it back to his accomplice. It does not appear that Signor Pistamiglio sold the turkeys; according to the most accredited version, he gave them as gifts to his lovers, who were numerous, old, ugly, and scattered throughout the foothills of the Piedmontese Alps.

But many, many stories were told; from what could be gathered, all fifty of the mine's inhabitants had reacted on each other, two by two, as in combinatorial analysis, that is to say, everyone with all the others, and especially every man with all the women, old maids or married, and every woman with all the men. All I had to do was select two names at random, better if of different sex, and ask a third person: 'What happened with those two?' and lo and behold, a splendid story was unfolded for me, since everyone knew the story of everyone else. It is not clear why these events, often quite complicated and always intimate, were told so offhandedly, particularly to me of all people, who on the contrary could tell nothing to anyone, not even my real name. But it appears but this is my fate (and

I'm definitely not complaining about it): I am one of those people to whom many things are told.

I recorded in various versions a remote saga going back to a period much before Signor Pistamiglio's. There had been a time when, in the mine's offices, they had had a real Gomorrah. During that legendary season, every evening, when the five-thirty siren sounded, none of the clerks went home. At that signal, liquor and mattresses suddenly popped up from among the desks, and an orgy erupted that embraced everything and everyone, young pubescent stenographers and balding accountants, starting with the then director all the way down to the disabled doorman: the sad round of mining paperwork gave way suddenly, every evening, to a boundless inter-class fornication, public and variously intertwined. No survivors had lived down to our day to provide direct testimony: a series of disastrous balance sheets had forced the board of governors in Milan to carry out a drastic, purifying intervention. Nobody except for Signora Bortolasso, who, I was assured, knew everything, had seen everything, but was not talking because of her extreme shyness.

Signora Bortolasso, in any case, never talked with anyone, outside the strict necessities of work. Before she had her present name she was called Gina delle Benne: at nineteen, already a typist in the office, she had fallen in love with a young, slim, red-headed miner who, without really reciprocating, showed himself nevertheless ready to accept her love; but her 'folks' had been adamant. They had spent money on her studies and she had to show her gratitude by making a good marriage and not hooking up with just anybody; and what's more, since the girl refused to be reasonable, they would see to it: either drop that redhead or get out of the house and the mine.

Gina was willing to wait until her twenty-first birthday (which was only two years away): but the redhead didn't wait for her. He showed up one Sunday with another woman, then with a third, and wound up marrying a fourth. Gina then made a cruel decision: if she couldn't bind herself to the man she cared for, the only one, well then, there would not be any other. Not a nun; she had modern ideas: but she forbade herself marriage forever in a refined and merciless manner, that is, by getting married. She was by now almost an executive, needed by the management, endowed with an iron memory and proverbial diligence: and she let everyone know, her parents and her bosses, that she intended to marry Bortolasso, the mine's simpleton.

This Bortolasso was a middle-aged laborer, strong as a mule and dirty as a pig. He most likely was not a real simpleton: it is more probable that he belonged to that species of human being of whom one says in Piedmont that they play the fool so as not to pay for the salt: sheltering behind the immunity granted the weak-minded, Bortolasso performed with extreme negligence the job of gardener – with a negligence that verged on rudimentary cunning. Very well, the world had declared him irresponsible and now it had to tolerate him as such, indeed give him a living and take care of him.

Asbestos drenched by rain is hard to extract, so the rain gauge at the mine was very important. It was placed in the middle of a flowerbed, and the director himself took the readings. Bortolasso, who every morning watered the flowerbed, got the habit of also watering the rain gauge, severely falsifying the data for the costs of extraction. The director (not immediately) realized this and gave him orders to stop. 'So then he likes it dry,' Bortolasso reasoned; and after every rain he would go and open the valve under the instrument.

When I arrived at the mine the situation had been stabilized for some time. Gina, now Signora Bortolasso, was about thirty-five: the modest beauty of her face had grown stiff and fixed in a tense, alert mask and bore the manifest stigma of a protracted virginity. For a virgin she had remained, they all knew it because Bortolasso told it to everyone. This had been the agreement at the time of the marriage; he had accepted it, even if later, almost every night, he tried to violate the woman's bed. But she had defended herself furiously and still defended herself – never, never would a man, and most of all that one, be permitted to touch her.

These nightly battles of the sad couple had become the talk of the mine, and one of its few attractions. On one of the first mild evenings, a group of aficionados invited me to come along with them to hear what happened. I refused and they returned disappointed soon after: they had heard only a trombone playing 'Faccetta Nera.'* They explained to me that sometimes this happened: he was a musical simpleton and would blow off steam in that way.

I fell in love with my work from the very first day, although it entailed nothing more at that stage than quantitative analysis of rock samples: attack with hydrofluoric acid, down comes iron with ammonia, down comes nickel (how little! a pinch of red sediment) with dimethylgloxyime, down comes magnesium with phosphate, always the same, every blessed day – in itself, it was not very stimulating. But stimulating and new was another sensation: the sample to be analyzed was no longer an anonymous, manufactured powder, a materialized quiz: it was a piece of rock, the earth's entrail, torn from the earth by the explosive's force; and on the basis of the daily data of the analysis little by little was born a map, the portrait of the subterranean veins. For the first time after seventeen years of schoolwork, of Greek verbs and the history of the Peloponnesian War, the things I had learned were beginning to be useful to me. Quantitative analysis, so devoid of emotion, heavy as granite, came alive, true, useful, when part of serious and concrete work. It was useful: it was part of a plan, a tessera in a mosaic. The analytical method I followed was no longer a bookish dogma, it was put to the test every day, it could be refined, made to conform with

* 'Little Black Face,' a Fascist song popularized at the time that Italy invaded Ethiopia, in 1936 – TRANS.

our aims, by a subtle play of reason, of trial and error. To make a mistake was no longer a vaguely comic accident that spoils an exam for you or affects your marks: to make a mistake was similar to when you go climbing – a contest, an act of attention, a step up that makes you more worthy and fit.

The girl in the lab was called Alida. She watched my neophyte's enthusiasms without sharing them; she was in fact surprised and somewhat annoyed. Her presence was not unpleasant. She was a *liceo* graduate, quoted Pindar and Sappho, the daughter of a completely innocuous small local Fascist official, was cunning and slothful, and didn't give a damn about anything, least of all the analysis of rock, which she had learned to perform mechanically from the lieutenant. She too, like all the people up there, had interacted with several persons and did not make a mystery of it with me, thanks to that curious gift for garnering confessions which I mentioned before. She had fought with many women because of vague rivalries, had fallen in love a little with many men, a great deal with one, and was engaged to still another, a gray, unpretentious fellow, an employee in the Technical Office who came from her town and whom her family had picked for her. About this, too, she didn't give a damn. What could she do about it? Rebel? Leave? No, she was a girl from a good family, her future was children and the kitchen stove, Sappho and Pindar were things of the past and nickel an abstruse stopgap. She worked listlessly in the lab while waiting for that so little longed-for marriage, negligently washing the precipitates, weighing the nickel-dimethylgloxyime, and I had hard work convincing her that it was not quite the thing to pad the results of the analyses: something she tended to do, in fact she confessed to having done often, since, she said, it didn't cost anybody anything, and pleased the director, the lieutenant, and myself.

What, after all, was that chemistry over which the lieutenant and I racked our brains? Water and fire, nothing else, like in the kitchen. A less appetizing kitchen, that's all: with penetrating or disgusting smells instead of the domestic kind; for the rest, there too aprons, mixing, burned hands, and washing up at the end of the day. No escape for Alida. She listened with devout compunction and at the same time Italian skepticism to my tales of life in Turin: these were heavily censored because in fact both she and I had to play the game of my anonymity. Nevertheless something did emerge: if nothing else, from my reticences themselves. After some weeks I realized that I was no longer a nameless person: I was a certain Doctor Levi who must not be called Levi, neither in the second nor the third person, due to good manners, and in order to avoid a mess. In the mine's gossipy and easygoing atmosphere, a disparity between my indeterminate state as an outcast and my visible mildness of manner leaped to the eye, and – Alida admitted this to me – was lengthily discussed and variously interpreted: I was everything from an agent of the OVRA, the Fascist secret police, to someone with high-class connections.

Going down into the valley was uncomfortable, and for me not very prudent; since I could not visit anyone, my evenings at the mine were interminable. Sometimes I stayed in the lab past quitting time or went back there after dinner to study, or to meditate on the problem of nickel. At other times I shut myself in to read Mann's Joseph stories in my monastic cell in the submarine. On nights when the moon was up I often took long solitary walks through the wild countryside around the mine, all the way up to the brim of the crater, or halfway up on the back of the gray, craggy dump chute, shaken by mysterious creaks and shivers as if some busy gnomes really nested there: the darkness was punctuated by the distant howls of dogs in the invisible valley bottom.

These roamings granted me a truce from the grim awareness of my father dying in Turin, of the American defeats at Bataan, the German victories in the Crimea, in short, of the open trap which was about to spring shut: it gave birth in me to a new bond, more sincere than the rhetoric about nature learned at school, with those brambles and stones which were my island and my freedom, a freedom I would perhaps soon lose.

For that rock without peace I felt a fragile and precarious affection: with it I had contracted a double bond, first in the exploits with Sandro, then here, trying as a chemist to wrest away its treasure. From this rocky love and these asbestos-filled solitudes, on some other of those long nights were born two stories of islands and freedom, the first I felt inclined to write after the torments of compositions in *liceo*: one story fantasized about a remote precursor of mine, a hunter of lead instead of nickel; the other, ambiguous and mercurial, I had taken from a reference to the island of Tristan da Cunha that I happened to see during that period.

The lieutenant, who was doing his military service in Turin, came up to the mine only one day a week. He would check my work and give me instructions and advice for the coming week, and proved to be an excellent chemist and a tenacious and acute researcher. After a short period of orientation, alongside the routine of daily analyses, a project with much higher aims began to take shape.

In the mine's rock there was indeed nickel, but very little: from our analyses it showed an average content of 0.2 percent. Ridiculous, in comparison to the minerals mined by my antipodal colleague-rivals in Canada and New Caledonia. But perhaps the raw material could be enriched? Under the lieutenant's guidance I tried all possible methods: by magnetic separation, by flotation, by levigation, by sifting, with heavy liquids, with the shaking plate. I did not get anywhere: nothing concentrated; in all the fractions the percentage of nickel remained obstinately the same as the first. Nature was not helping us: we concluded that the nickel accompanying the bivalent iron took its place vicariously, followed it like an evanescent shadow, a minuscule brother: 0.2 percent of nickel, 8 percent of iron. All the reagents imaginable for nickel should have been employed in doses forty times greater, even without taking into account the magnesium. An economically desperate enterprise. At moments of weariness I perceived the rock that encircled me, the green serpentine of the Alpine foothills, in all its sidereal, hostile, extraneous hardness: in comparison, the trees of the valley, by now already dressed for spring, were like us, also people who do not speak but feel the heat and the frost, enjoy and suffer, are born and die, fling out pollen with the wind, obscurely follow the sun in its travels. Not the rock: it does not house any energy, it is extinguished since primordial times, pure hostile passivity; a massive fortress that I had to pull down bastion by bastion to get my hands on the hidden sprite, the capricious *kupfernickel* which jumps out now here, now there, elusive and malign, with long perked ears, always ready to flee from the blows of the investigating pickax, leaving you with nothing to show for it.

But this is no longer the time for sprites, *nickel*, and kobolds. We are chemists, that is, hunters: ours are 'the two experiences of adult life' of which Pavese spoke, success and failure, to kill the white whale or wreck the ship; one should not surrender to incomprehensible matter, one must not just sit down. We are here for this – to make mistakes and to correct ourselves, to stand the blows and hand them out. We must never feel disarmed: nature is immense and complex, but it is not impermeable to the intelligence; we must circle around it, pierce and probe it, look for the opening or make it. My weekly conversations with the lieutenant sounded like war plans.

Among the many attempts we had made there also was that of reducing the rock with hydrogen. We had placed the mineral, finely ground, in a porcelain boat; had placed this in turn in a quartz tube; and through the tube, heated from the outside, we had pushed a current of hydrogen in the hope that this would strip the oxygen bound to the nickel and leave it reduced, that is, naked, in its metallic state. Metallic nickel, like iron, is magnetic, and therefore, according to this hypothesis, it would have been easy to separate it from the rest, alone or with the iron, simply by means of a small magnet. But, after the treatment, we had vainly agitated a powerful magnet in the watery suspension of our powder: we had only gotten a trace of iron. Clear and sad: hydrogen, under these conditions, did not reduce anything; the nickel, together with the iron, must be firmly lodged in the serpentine's structure, combined with the silicate and water, satisfied (so to speak) with its state and averse to assuming another.

But say one tried to pull that structure apart. The idea came to me as one switches on a light, one day when by chance there fell into my hands an old dusty diagram, the work of some unknown predecessor of mine; it showed the loss of weight in the mine's asbestos as a function of temperature. The asbestos lost a little water at 150° centigrade, then remained apparently unaltered until about 800° centigrade;

here one noted an abrupt step down with a fall in weight of 12 percent, and the author had remarked: 'becomes fragile.' Now serpentine is the father of asbestos: if asbestos decomposes at 800° centigrade, serpentine should do so also; and, since a chemist does not think, indeed does not live, without models, I idly went about representing them for myself, drawing on paper long chains of silicon, oxygen, iron, and magnesium, with a little nickel caught between their links, and then the same chains after the smash reduced to short stubs, with the nickel flushed out of its den and exposed to attack; and I did not feel much different from the remote hunter of Altamira who painted an antelope on the rock wall so that the next day's hunt would be lucky.

The propitiatory ceremonies did not last long: the lieutenant was not there, but he could arrive from one hour to the next, and I was afraid that he would not accept, or would not readily accept, my very unorthodox hypothesis of work. But I felt it itch all over my skin: what's done is done, best get to work immediately.

There is nothing more vivifying than a hypothesis. Watched with an amused and skeptical expression by Alida, who, since it was now late in the afternoon, kept looking ostentatiously at her wristwatch, I set to work like a whirlwind. In a moment the apparatus was mounted, the thermostat set at 800° centigrade, the pressure regulator on the tank set, the fluxmeter put in order. I heated the material for half an hour, then reduced the temperature and passed the hydrogen through for another hour: by now it was dark, the girl had gone, all was silence against the backdrop of the grim hum of the Grading Department, which also worked at night. I felt part conspirator, part alchemist.

When the time came, I took the porcelain boat out of the quartz tube, let it cool off in the vacuum, then dispersed in water the powder, which had turned from greenish to a dirty yellow: a thing which seemed to me a good sign. I picked up the magnet and set to work. Each time I took the magnet out of the water, it brought with it a tuft of brown powder: I removed it delicately with filter paper and put it aside, perhaps a milligram each time; for the analysis to be well-founded at least a half gram of material was needed, that is, several hours of work. I decided to stop about midnight: to interrupt the separation, I mean to say, because at no cost would I have put off the beginning of the analysis. For this, since it involved a magnetic fraction (and therefore presumably poor in silicates), and yielding to my haste, I there and then tried a simplified variant. At three in the morning I had the result: no longer the usual pink little cloud of nickel-dimethylgloxyime but rather a visibly abundant precipitate. Filtered, washed, dried, and weighed. The final datum appeared to me written in letters of fire on the slide rule: 6 percent of nickel, the rest iron. A victory: even without a further separation, an alloy to be sent to the electric oven as is. I returned to the submarine when it was almost dawn with an acute desire to go immediately and wake the director, telephone the lieutenant, and roll around on the dark fields, which were dripping wet with dew. I was thinking many foolish things, and I was not thinking of anything sensible and sad.

I was thinking of having opened a door with a key, and of possessing the key to many doors, perhaps to all of them. I was thinking of having thought of something that nobody else had yet thought, not even in Canada or New Caledonia, and I felt invincible and untouchable even when faced by close enemies, closer each month. Finally, I was thinking of having had a far from ignoble revenge on those who had declared me biologically inferior.

I was not thinking that if the method of extraction I had caught sight of could have found industrial application, the nickel produced would have entirely ended up in Fascist Italy's and Hitler Germany's armor plate and artillery shells. I was not thinking that during those very months there had been discovered in Albania deposits of nickel mineral before which ours could go and hide, and along with it every project of mine, the director's, and the lieutenant's. I did not foresee that my interpretation of the magnetic separability of nickel was substantially mistaken, as the lieutenant showed me a few days later, as soon as I told him of my results. Nor did I foresee that the director, after having shared my enthusiasm for a few days, threw a wet blanket on mine and his when he realized that there did not exist in commerce any magnetic selector capable of separating a material in the form of a fine powder, and that on cruder powders my method could not function.

And yet this story does not end here. Despite the many years that have passed, the liberalization of exchanges, and the fall in the international price of nickel, the news of the enormous wealth that lies in that valley in the form of rubble accessible to everyone still sets fire to the imagination. Not far from the mine, in cellars, stables, on the borderline between chemistry and white magic, there are still people who go at night to the rubble heaps and come back with bags of gray gravel, grind it, cook it, treat it with ever new reagents. The fascination of buried wealth, of two kilos of a noble silvery metal bound to a thousand kilos of sterile stone which is thrown away, has not yet died out.

POCKET PENGUINS

POCKET PENGUINS